the Lion

by **ANDREW STARK** illustrated by **EMILY FAITH JOHNSON**

PICTURE WINDOW BOOKS
a capstone imprint

Published by Picture Window Books, an imprint of Capstone.
1710 Roe Crest Drive, North Mankato, Minnesota 56003
capstonepub.com

Library of Congress Cataloging-in-Publication Data

Names: Stark, Andrew (Ojibwa Indian), author. | Johnson, Emily Faith, illustrator.
Title: Liam the lion / by Andrew Stark ; illustrated by Emily Faith Johnson.
Description: North Mankato, Minnesota : Picture Window Books, an imprint of Capstone, [2023] | Series: Liam Kingbird's kingdom | Audience: Ages 5-7. | Audience: Grades K-1. | Summary: Liam is an Ojibwa boy starting at a new school, and he is self conscious because of his cleft lip—especially after another boy tells him that he looks like a lion.
Identifiers: LCCN 2022041480 (print) | LCCN 2022041481 (ebook) | ISBN 9781666395051 (hardcover) | ISBN 9781484670538 (paperback) | ISBN 9781484670545 (pdf) | ISBN 9781484683347 (kindle edition)
Subjects: LCSH: Ojibwa Indian—Juvenile fiction. | Cleft lip—Juvenile fiction. | Self confidence—Juvenile fiction. | Self-consciousness (Sensitivity)—Juvenile fiction. | CYAC: Ojibwa Indians—Fiction. | Cleft lip—Fiction. | Self-confidence—Fiction. | Self-consciousness—Fiction. | LCGFT: Fiction.
Classification: LCC PZ7.1.S73758 Lk 2023 (print) | LCC PZ7.1.S73758 (ebook) | DDC 813.6 [Fic]—dc23/eng/20220830
LC record available at https://lccn.loc.gov/2022041480
LC ebook record available at https://lccn.loc.gov/2022041481

Designer:
Tracy Davies

Design Elements:
Shutterstock: Daria Dyk, Oksancia, Rainer Lesniewski

Printed and bound in the USA. 5195

Table of Contents

MEET LIAM KINGBIRD!

Liam loves to draw!

Liam has a cleft lip.

Liam is Ojibwa.

Liam is a good thinker.

Liam speaks two languages.

Liam likes animals.

WHAT MAKES YOU SPECIAL?

Chapter 1

A WHISPER

Liam was a shy boy. He didn't know where this shyness had come from. It had always been there, like a small voice whispering from his shadow.

Whenever Liam went somewhere new, his heart would race and his face would feel hot. Sometimes, he would get very quiet.

Today was a quiet day. Liam's
mom was driving him to a new
school on the Ojibwa Indian
Reservation.

"What's wrong?" his mom asked.

Liam shrugged. "I guess I'm
nervous."

"You know," she said, "sometimes nervousness can be confused with excitement. Maybe you're really excited. That's a good thing."

Liam thought about this. Then he smiled. Maybe it was excitement he felt.

When they arrived, Liam could see the other kids walking into school. They all seemed to know each other already.

"You'll do great, Liam," his mom said. "You're a very special boy."

"How am I special?" Liam asked.

"Because, you create entire worlds with your drawings, and you have the wildest imagination I've ever seen," she said.

Liam laughed. "Thanks, Mom. But you can't see an imagination."

"I see it when you draw!" she said. She leaned over, kissed his head, and whispered, "Gi-zaagi'in."

"I love you too," Liam said.

Chapter 2

LIAM THE BRAVE

Compared to Liam's old

school, this one seemed huge.

Each hallway looked like it went

on forever.

The principal, Mrs. Loonsfoot,

was really friendly.

"And you must be Liam!" she said. "Let's take you down to Mrs. Dakota's third-grade class."

There were a lot of kids in Mrs. Dakota's class. Liam counted at least fifteen. They all looked at Liam when he walked in.

"Good morning, everyone!" Mrs. Loonsfoot said. "This is Liam Kingbird. Let's all join together with a big, loud, 'Welcome, Liam!'"

"Welcome, Liam!" the kids yelled.

Liam noticed that a few of the kids didn't say anything.

● ● ●

Outside at recess, Liam kept to himself. He sat on a swing, but he wasn't swinging. Instead, Liam kicked at the sand, pretending not to watch the other kids play.

One boy walked over after jumping down from the monkey bars.

"Hey," he said. "I'm Jeremy."

"Hi," Liam said. "My name's Liam."

"What's wrong with your mouth?" Jeremy said.

Liam looked up at him. "Nothing."

"It's funny," Jeremy said. "Your lip is funny."

Liam looked away. "What's funny about it?"

Jeremy said, "You look like a lion."

Liam could hear the voice in his shadow whispering, and he felt his face get very hot.

●●●

After Liam's mom picked him up from school, he was quiet again on the drive home.

"What's wrong, honey?" she asked. "How did it go today?"

Liam started to cry.

Liam's mom pulled the car into a parking lot. Then she took Liam's hand in hers.

"Tell me what happened," she said.

Liam wiped his eyes with the back of his hand.

"A boy named Jeremy made fun of me. He said my lip is funny. He said I look like a lion," Liam said.

"You don't look like a lion, honey," his mom said. "But you sure act like one."

Liam looked up at her.

"You're brave like a lion," she said. "You carry the strength of a lion in your heart."

He wiped his eyes again. "What do you mean?"

"What are lions known for?" she asked.

Liam thought for a moment. "Being strong?"

His mom nodded. "That's right. I think your spirit animal is a lion."

Liam pictured a strong, brave, and powerful lion. He smiled.

Chapter 3

A ROAR

The next day, Mrs. Dakota was teaching a lesson about Africa. She had big pictures of all kinds of fascinating animals up on the board.

"Can anyone tell me what kind of bird this is?" she asked.

The class was silent.

"It's called a shoebill," Mrs. Dakota said, pointing to the bird's beak, "because its beak looks like a shoe."

Everybody laughed.

The next one was a picture of a lion. Jeremy turned around and looked at Liam. Liam felt his face get hot again.

"And we all know what this—"

"Lion!" The class interrupted
Mrs. Dakota.

"That's right," she said,
laughing. "King of the Jungle!"

"King of the Jungle!" the
students repeated.

Jeremy said, "That's Liam! Because he looks like a lion. And he has 'king' in his name! Liam the Lion!"

Everybody turned around and looked at Liam. Liam stared down at his desk.

"Liam the Lion! Liam the Lion!" his classmates echoed.

"King Liam!" one girl said. "King Liam!"

"Liam's King of the Jungle!" Jeremy cheered.

Liam peeked up at his classmates.

"King Liam! King Liam!" the class chanted. "King Liam!"

Liam was not nervous. He was not hot. He was proud! He smiled. For a moment, that little voice from his shadow did not whisper—it roared. For a moment, Liam was king.

FACTS ABOUT OJIBWA

WHAT'S IN A NAME?

The Ojibwa are Indigenous people also known as Ojibwe, Chippewa, Anishinaabe, and Salteaux, depending on where they live. Many live in southern Canada and in the northern Midwest and the northern Plains of the United States.

"BOOZHOO! HELLO!"

The Ojibwa speak an Algonquian language called Anishinaabemowin or Ojibwemowin, which are dialects that change slightly from region to region. Dialect includes word pronunciation, grammar, and vocabulary. Most speakers of Ojibwemowin live in parts of Michigan, Wisconsin, Minnesota, or southern Canada. A school in Wisconsin is called the Waadookodaading Ojibwe Language Immersion School. All of its classes are taught in the Ojibwa language.

A LONG, LONG TIME AGO . . .

The earliest Ojibwa stories were either handed down through oral histories or birch bark scrolls. These stories tell of the five original Ojibwa clans, or doodem. These were the Bullhead Fish (Wawaazisii), Crane (Baswenaazhi), Pintail Duck (Aan'aawenh), Bear (Nooke), and Little Moose (Moozoonsii). There was a sixth doodem, the Thunderbird (Animikii), but he was too powerful and had to return to the ocean.

WHAT'S FOR DINNER?

Today the Ojibwa live very much like many other Americans and Canadians and eat what they do. But the original Ojibwa people were hunters and gatherers. They survived on wild rice and corn, lots of fish, and small game like squirrels and rabbits.

OJIBWA KIDS: JUST LIKE YOU

In the past, Ojibwa kids played with handmade dolls and toys. Lacrosse was a popular sport among older children. Today Ojibwa kids go to school, play sports and video games, and hang out with their friends. However, many are still very connected to the outdoors and love to go hunting and fishing.

GLOSSARY

cleft lip (KLEFT LIP)—a condition in which the lip does not fully form before birth, resulting in a gap or opening in the lip; surgery can close the gap and may leave a small scar on the upper lip

confuse (kun-FYOOZ)—to mix up

fascinating (FASS-uh-nay-ting)—very interesting or attention-getting

interrupt (in-ter-UPT)—to speak over someone else

nervous (NER-vuss)—feeling scared or unsure

reservation (rez-ur-VAY-shun)—land reserved for Indigenous tribal nations; in the past, many Indigenous people were forcibly moved to reservations by the United States government

shoebill (SHOO-bill)—a large gray wading bird that lives in wetlands in eastern Africa

GIVE IT SOME THOUGHT

- Starting a new school can be exciting. It can also be scary. Have you ever started a new school or activity? What did you do to feel brave?

- Feeling strong and brave like a lion makes Liam proud. Draw a picture of your favorite animal. Below your picture, write a list of the animal's special qualities. Is it fast? Can it fly? What qualities do you admire about this animal?

- When Liam met Jeremy on the playground, what did Jeremy say that hurt Liam's feelings? Even if Jeremy didn't mean to be hurtful, it felt that way to Liam. Can you think of a different way Jeremy might have introduced himself?

- Gi-zaagi'in (gee-zah-gee-IN) means "I love you" in Ojibwa. Can you say "I love you" in other languages?

ABOUT THE CREATORS

Andrew Stark was raised on the Ojibwa Indian Reservation in Michigan's Upper Peninsula. After earning his MFA from Pacific University, he moved to Los Angeles and began his career as an editor for a fashion magazine. He has since been published in a variety of publications, and one of his short stories was adapted into a stage play. He lives in Saint Paul, Minnesota, with his two dogs—Gizmo, a Chihuahua, and Barney, a chiweenie. Together, they love to camp and go hiking.

Emily Faith Johnson grew up on a farm in northern Wisconsin. She is a graphic designer, writer, and illustrator who loves bringing characters to life through her artwork. She's always secretly wanted to become a Broadway star, so when she's not writing or making art, you can usually find her serenading her goats and ponies with show tunes. She is a member of the Sault Ste. Marie Tribe of Chippewa Indians.